Playing Hooky

Once they made their way through the crowd, the three girls started to run. They didn't have a moment to lose. Elizabeth was going so fast that she nearly tripped. When she steadied herself, she found herself looking straight into a familiar face. It was the principal's secretary, Mrs. Knight, staring right at her!

"Oh, no. Do you see who I see?" Lila said, groaning.

Jessica's heart sank when she caught sight of Mrs. Knight through the crowd. "She's going to go right to Mr. Clark. We're in for it now."

SWEET VALLEY TWINS

Playing Hooky

Written by
Jamie Suzanne

Created by
FRANCINE PASCAL

A BANTAM SKYLARK BOOK®
TORONTO · NEW YORK · LONDON · SYDNEY · AUCKLAND

RL 4 008–12

PLAYING HOOKY
A Bantam Skylark Book / July 1988

Skylark Books is a registered trademark of Bantam Books,
a division of Bantam Doubleday Dell Publishing Group, Inc.
Registered in U.S. Patent and Trademark Office and elsewhere.

Sweet Valley High® and Sweet Valley Twins are
trademarks of Francine Pascal

Conceived by Francine Pascal

Produced by Daniel Weiss Associates, Inc.,
27 West 20th Street, New York, N.Y. 10011

Cover art by James Mathewuse

ISBN 0-553-15606-3

Published simultaneously in the United States and Canada

Bantam Books are published by Bantam Books, a division of Bantam
Doubleday Dell Publishing Group, Inc. Its trademark, consisting of the
words "Bantam Books" and the portrayal of a rooster, is Registered in
U.S. Patent and Trademark Office and in other countries. Marca Regis-
trada. Bantam Books, 666 Fifth Avenue, New York, New York 10103.

PRINTED IN THE UNITED STATES OF AMERICA

O   0 9 8 7 6 5 4

To
Larry Smith

One
◇

"Well, Lizzie? What do you think? Are these sneakers the greatest, or what?"

Jessica Wakefield jumped up and held her left foot high in the air. Elizabeth took one look at the purple sneaker her twin was waving directly in front of her nose and made a face.

"Ugh, Jessica. Those are the most hideous sneakers I've ever seen!"

It was Friday evening, and Jessica was in the middle of an all-out shopping spree at the Sweet Valley Mall. She brought her foot down and placed her hands on her hips. She was used to having disagreements with her twin. From their long, sun-streaked blond hair and sparkling blue-green eyes to the tiny dimples on their left cheeks it was almost impossible to tell them apart. But when it came to their taste in friends, clothes, and hobbies, they were really quite different.

Elizabeth, the older by four minutes, was the more levelheaded. She often joked about being the older sister, and most of the time Elizabeth did act more grown up. She liked having long talks with her friends, reading books, and writing for the class newspaper, the *Sweet Valley Sixers*. Jessica was more happy-go-lucky. Gossiping about boys and discussing the latest fashions with her friends were among her favorite activities.

"You're kidding, aren't you, Elizabeth?" she cried. "These sneakers are perfect."

Elizabeth tried to force a frown, then burst out laughing. It was no use. Once Jessica had her mind made up, there was no way to change it.

Jessica quickly unlaced the purple sneakers, put them back in the box, and got in line at the cash register. Elizabeth stood patiently beside her. "This is just what we need to win that basketball game next week—special purple sneakers for the star player. Besides, the Unicorns will flip when they see these." The Unicorn Club was a group of girls who thought they were as beautiful and as special as the mythical beast for which they were named. And they wore something purple every day.

Elizabeth smiled. "You're so modest, Jess." It was true, though. Jessica was easily the best player on the sixth-grade team. She had been one of the first to join the team when the sign-up sheets were posted, and she'd already helped lead the team to five straight victories.

"I can't believe Tracy Dyer had the nerve to quit the Booster squad so late in the season," Jessica said as the girls waited in the long line. She had been complaining about it ever since Tracy had announced that her family was moving to New York.

"Jess, don't you think you're being a little unfair to Tracy?" Elizabeth said. "She didn't decide to move. Her parents did, and besides, moving across the country and having to make all new friends isn't going to be easy."

"I guess it isn't," Jessica admitted. "But now we have to fill her spot on the squad. With me playing basketball, and Tracy gone, there aren't too many Boosters left."

"C'mon, Jess, it's not that bad," Elizabeth said.

"Look on the bright side. You might find somebody really good. You might even be able to sign up another Unicorn member."

"I doubt it," Jessica muttered.

A few minutes later, the twins were still waiting to pay. Suddenly they heard a familiar voice.

"Jessica! Jessica!" It was Lila Fowler calling from the entryway. She was practically out of breath when she reached the girls. She gave Elizabeth a quick hello, then turned to Jessica. "You've got to come with me—right away."

Jessica knew that Lila sometimes overreacted, but this time she really seemed excited. "What is it, Lila? Is it really important?"

"Does the name Kent Kellerman mean anything to you?" Lila demanded.

Jessica and Elizabeth knew the name at once. Sixteen-year-old Kent Kellerman was the cutest boy on TV. The twins and their friends never missed an episode of "All the World," the popular show he starred in.

Both girls had heard that Kent would be in Sweet Valley sometime soon to do some on-location filming. The worst part was finding out that the filming would take place on a school day.

"Well, everyone is running down to the other end of the mall screaming Kent's name," Lila said. "If we want to find out what's going on we'd better hurry. Maybe they changed his schedule."

Jessica turned to Elizabeth with an innocent look in her eyes. "Lizzie," Jessica began in her sweetest voice, "if one of us doesn't stand in line, I won't be able to get my new sneakers and . . ."

Elizabeth sighed. "Don't worry, Jess. I'll stay here," she said. "Just don't forget we've got to meet Mom outside the Valley Cinema at nine on the button." But Jessica and Lila were already halfway out the store by the time she finished talking.

"Hi, Elizabeth," she heard someone say.

Elizabeth turned to see that Brooke Dennis had joined the line behind her. She had a new pair of leather riding boots in her hands. "Hi, Brooke." Elizabeth was surprised to see someone her own age still at this end of the mall. "Aren't you going to see Kent Kellerman? He's supposedly down at the other end of the mall."

Brooke tucked a stray lock of light brown hair behind her ear and shook her head. "Oh, he's not here," she said. "It's just a poster they're putting up advertising his show. They're going to be filming scenes for it in Sweet Valley on Monday. My father will be working on the show." Brooke's father was a famous Hollywood screenwriter.

"You never told me your father worked with Kent."

"I know. I haven't told too many people because I'm afraid everybody would want to meet Kent. If I introduced one person, I'd have to introduce the whole class."

"I guess that could be a real problem," Elizabeth admitted. "Does your father spend a lot of time with Kent?"

"I guess so," Brooke mumbled. "He talks to Kent more than he talks to me these days."

"Well, I guess the show must keep your father pretty busy," Elizabeth said, noticing Brooke's sad expression as they walked out of the shoe store.

"That's for sure. He's been working night and day for the past five weeks," Brooke said. Elizabeth could see tears brimming in Brooke's eyes. Brooke's parents had divorced a few years ago and her mother now lived in Europe.

Elizabeth reached out and patted Brooke on the shoulder. "It's all right, Brooke," she said. "I think I know how you feel. Both my parents work and sometimes when I come home from school and no one is there it feels pretty lonely."

Brooke wiped a tear off her cheek with the back of her hand.

"Hey, I have a great idea," Elizabeth said cheerfully. "Let's go have a Super-Double Banana Split Special at Casey's Place!" She led Brooke through the mall toward the old-fashioned ice-cream parlor, one of her favorite spots.

A few minutes later, they sat down at one of the glass-topped tables and ordered the special to share. They ate the ice cream in silence until they had finished every last drop. Elizabeth sighed and sat back in her chair. "I think I'm about to burst."

"Ugh, me, too," Brooke said with a groan. "I feel like I ate the whole thing myself. Are you sure you shared it with me?"

"I was going to ask you the same thing. I'm not even sure I can stand up," Elizabeth said, licking the last drop of butterscotch sauce from her spoon.

Brooke giggled, and Elizabeth was relieved that she seemed to be feeling better.

"Hey, you know what?" Elizabeth said suddenly. "I've been so busy since I joined the basketball team that I haven't had much time for the paper. How would you like to help me out? We could use another staff member."

"Me?" Brooke asked, looking surprised. "I've never done anything like that before."

"Well, there's always a first time, right?" Elizabeth said.

"Yes. I guess so," Brooke said. "I read the *Sweet Valley Sixers* every week, but I never thought about working on it. What could I do?"

"You could take photographs if you've got a camera," Elizabeth said. "Or you could write an article."

"Maybe I could do an interview or something like that," Brooke suggested. "That would be neat."

Elizabeth grinned. It was as if Brooke had read her mind. "I've got just the assignment for you. The ballet is coming to town this weekend. Have you ever heard of Kate DiNardo, the director of the company that's coming?"

"Heard of her!" Brooke exclaimed. "She's a world-famous ballerina!"

Elizabeth nodded. "She used to be one of Madame André's students. Every year she comes back to Sweet Valley and gives a free outdoor performance at Secca Lake."

"Wow!" Brooke said. "I'd love to meet her."

"Well, now's your chance!" Elizabeth said. "I set up an appointment with her for this coming Tuesday. How would you like to conduct the interview?"

Brooke was quiet for a minute. "I don't know," she finally said. "I think I'd be so nervous I wouldn't know what to ask."

"We could write up a list of questions to ask her," Elizabeth suggested.

"I don't know what to say," Brooke finally blurted out.

"Say you'll do it." Elizabeth smiled.

"OK, I'll do it," said Brooke with a grin.

By the time Elizabeth reached the Valley Cinema, Jessica was already sitting in their family's maroon van, waiting impatiently. Mrs. Wakefield was behind the wheel, glancing at her watch.

"Well, nice of you to show up," Jessica said as Elizabeth climbed in and shut the door.

"What happened, honey?" Mrs. Wakefield asked. "Did you get stuck in line somewhere?"

"Actually," Elizabeth admitted, "I was talking to Brooke Dennis and forgot all about the time. Brooke's going to write an article for the *Sweet Valley Sixers* next week. I'm sorry I kept you waiting, but she was pretty upset. I thought that getting her involved with something new might make her feel better."

"That's wonderful, dear," Mrs. Wakefield said.

As they drove through the quaint downtown section of Sweet Valley, Elizabeth noticed that Jessica was unusually quiet.

"So," Elizabeth asked, "did you get to meet Kent Kellerman?"

Jessica shook her head. "He wasn't there. It was

just a sign advertising his show. It's hopeless anyway," Jessica said, looking glum. "Not only is the filming taking place during school, but Lila says Kent will probably have bodyguards all around him."

"She's probably right. Did you know Brooke Dennis's father is working on the show?" Elizabeth asked.

Jessica turned to her twin with her mouth wide open. "Are you kidding? Mr. Dennis knows Kent Kellerman personally?" Jessica cried. "I'll bet he could introduce us to Kent!"

Jessica went on and on and by the time they got home, Elizabeth had just about had it with Jessica and all her chattering about Kent.

"I'll bet Brooke would ask her father to help us meet Kent," Jessica said. "I think I'll call her right now."

"Forget it, Jess," Elizabeth said. Her tone was firm. "Brooke said she didn't want word to get out that her father worked on the show. She knows the whole school will bother her about it."

Jessica frowned. "I won't invite the whole school, Elizabeth, just the Unicorns." She made a dash for the phone.

"Jess, please!" Elizabeth exclaimed. "I told Brooke I wouldn't tell anyone about it. Promise me you won't ask her to introduce you to Kent."

Jessica didn't answer.

"Jessica?" Elizabeth said in her older-sister voice.

"All right, I promise," Jessica finally mumbled. She walked into the bathroom that separated the twins' rooms and gazed at herself in the mirror. "But wouldn't it be great to meet him? He's *so* cute and— I'll bet he's —" Jessica saw the frown on her sister's face and stopped.

"You promised, Jess," Elizabeth reminded her twin.

"Can't I even think about him?" Jessica pleaded.

Elizabeth laughed and shook her head. "You're incredible, Jess."

"All right, don't worry," Jessica muttered as she walked into her bedroom. "I won't say anything to Brooke. You've got my word."

As she lay in bed that night, Jessica couldn't stop thinking about Kent Kellerman. *It isn't fair*, she said to herself as she tossed and turned, unable to fall asleep. *My favorite TV star comes to Sweet Valley and I'm not going to get so much as a glimpse of him. Unless . . .*

Jessica's heart started to pound. She had a brilliant idea. *What if I could make Brooke want to help us meet him?*

She had promised Elizabeth that she wouldn't ask Brooke, but what if Brooke volunteered to help them meet Kent? It wouldn't be easy, but Jessica knew she could figure out a way to make it work.

Drifting off to sleep moments later, she had the most wonderful dream. She and Kent were on the beach at sunset. Kent held her hand and gave her a gentle kiss on the cheek. "You're beautiful, Jessica," he said in a dreamy voice. "Every bit as pretty as Brooke said you were. I have a feeling we're going to be very good friends." As Jessica fell into a deeper sleep, she vowed to make her dream come true.

Two

◇

"You're not going to believe the incredible news I've got," Jessica whispered.

It was Saturday morning and Jessica had gotten up before anyone so she could call Lila.

"Let me guess," Lila said in a sleepy voice. "You bought those purple and white earrings on sale at Valley Fashions?"

"No!" Jessica said impatiently. "It's about Kent Kellerman."

"I know already," Lila said. "He's coming to town on Monday and we won't see him."

"Don't be so sure about that!" Jessica exclaimed.

"What do you mean?" Lila asked, suddenly sounding wide-awake.

"First of all," Jessica said, "it's a secret. And it's got to stay that way."

"I can keep a secret. What's the big news?"

"Brooke Dennis's father is working on Kent's show," Jessica whispered. "He can probably get passes to the set. We could meet Kent!"

Lila gasped. "Are you sure?"

"Positive," Jessica said. "But Brooke doesn't want anyone to bother her about meeting Kent. I had to promise Elizabeth I wouldn't say anything to her."

"So what good is knowing all this if we can't ask her to get us on the set?" Lila asked.

"Well, I have an idea," Jessica said. "What if we make her want to help us meet him?"

Lila paused. "How are we supposed to do that?"

"What if we offered her a spot on the Booster squad?" Jessica said. "She might want to show us how thankful she was with a couple of set passes to see Kent."

"What makes you think she wants to join the Boosters?" Lila asked.

Jessica paused to make sure no one was coming downstairs. "Elizabeth told me that Brooke has been looking for some activity to do after school. The

Boosters would be perfect. Besides, what girl wouldn't kill to be on the squad? She'll be so flattered that we asked her. All we'll have to do is mention Kent's name and I'm sure she'll volunteer."

"That makes sense," Lila agreed. "You really think it will work?"

"Trust me," Jessica said.

"She doesn't *really* have to make the squad, though, does she?" Lila said. "I mean, I like Brooke, but I really don't think she's Booster material."

"Of course not," Jessica replied. "Just as long as she feels like she has a chance. That way she'll want to show us how grateful she feels."

Jessica was suddenly startled by a noise upstairs. Elizabeth might be waking up. There was no time to explain the rest of her plan now. "Stay by your phone," she whispered to Lila. "I'll call you later."

"Hey, you two," Steven Wakefield shouted to Elizabeth and Jessica. It was later that morning and the twins were practicing on the basketball court in their driveway. "If you want to be able to play basketball, you're going to have to learn from an expert."

"Gee," Elizabeth teased. "If you see any experts around, let us know!"

"Ha, ha, ha!" Steven snorted. "Very funny." Tall and athletic, fourteen-year-old Steven was the twins' older brother and one of the best basketball players on the Sweet Valley High team. He ran onto the court with his hands out in front of him, ready to catch the ball.

Jessica passed him the ball as he glided toward the hoop that hung over the garage door. Steven bounced the ball twice, then banked it off the back-board for two points. He raised his arms in a victory salute to himself and mimicked the roar of the crowd.

"C'mon, Steven, are you going to help us out or not?" Jessica complained. "We haven't got all day to watch you congratulate yourself."

Steven finished prancing around the court and stood in front of the girls with a serious look on his face. Jessica and Elizabeth waited patiently while he looked them over like a general inspecting his troops.

"You," Steven boomed as he pointed to Jessica. "Front and center!" Jessica, playing along reluctantly, rolled her eyes and stepped forward, standing at attention. Steven pointed at Jessica's brand-new purple sneakers. "If you want to be a real basketball player, those sneakers will have to go. They're the ugliest things I've ever seen!"

Elizabeth tried to hold back her laughter as she watched her twin's mouth drop open.

"Steven Wakefield," Jessica cried, "you are the biggest creep ever to crawl out from under a rock!" Steven dropped the ball and doubled over with laughter. Jessica quickly scooped it up and got ready to throw it at her brother in anger. He was still laughing uncontrollably. "You've got three seconds to get out of here, you creep!" Jessica yelled. "One . . . two. . . three!" She flung her arm forward, but the ball slipped and bounced harmlessly to rest in front of Steven.

Steven picked it up and dribbled around Jessica with lightning speed. "Wow, you really do need my help. You can't even make a good pass." With that he grinned at his sisters, took a shot from the foul line, and walked off before the ball fell through the net with a swish.

Elizabeth walked over to her twin. "Don't listen to him, Jess. One thing he doesn't need is practice at being a pain."

"You're right, Lizzie," Jessica said. "We don't need his help anyway."

The sun was almost directly overhead by the time the twins stopped for a break. Elizabeth was just beginning to catch on to the reverse lay-up Jessica was teaching her. "I don't know how you do it, Jess," she said as they walked toward the house. "It looks like you've been playing basketball your whole life."

"Thanks, Lizzie. You're getting pretty good, too," she said encouragingly. "Soon everyone will be comparing you to the great Jessica Wakefield!"

The two girls laughed as they opened the back door and headed into the kitchen for something to drink.

"It looks like Sweet Valley has another star player in the making," Mrs. Wakefield said when the twins stepped inside. She removed a pitcher of lemonade from the refrigerator and filled two glasses. "I thought you two were going to be out there until dark."

"Jessica was trying to teach me some of her fancy moves," Elizabeth said. She took a sip of the ice-cold lemonade. "I'm not sure she succeeded."

"That's not true, Lizzie," Jessica exclaimed. "You were doing great. You may even give me some competition for Most Valuable Player."

Mrs. Wakefield gave each of the girls a hug as she headed for the door. "I've got some errands to run, girls. I'll see you two later."

She was almost out the door when she stopped and turned around. "Oh, Elizabeth, by the way, Julie Porter called. She wanted to remind you to come to her house at noon."

Elizabeth looked at the clock. It was already almost noon. "Oh, my gosh! I've got to hurry!" She gulped down the rest of her lemonade and jumped up from the table.

"What's so important, Liz?" Jessica asked.

"Brooke is meeting us at Julie's house today to discuss the article she's writing for the paper."

"She's meeting you at Julie's today?" Jessica asked, her eyes widening. If Elizabeth and Julie succeeded in getting Brooke to join the paper, her plan would be useless. Brooke wouldn't have time for both the newspaper *and* the Boosters.

"Yes," Elizabeth said. "Why?"

"Oh, nothing," Jessica replied casually.

But once Elizabeth had disappeared upstairs, Jessica dashed into their father's office and picked up the phone. She quickly dialed Brooke's number. There was no answer. She must be on her way to Julie's already.

Jessica picked up the phone again, this time calling Lila. "Meet me at the Dairi Burger in ten minutes," she whispered when Lila answered. "Brooke's on her way to Julie's right this minute. We've got to talk to her before they do. It's our only chance!"

Jessica hung up the phone and took a deep breath. Brooke lived just a few blocks from Julie. She was going to have to hurry. She darted out the front door, hoping she wasn't too late.

Brooke was just walking up the path to Julie's house when Jessica turned the corner.

"Brooke!" Jessica called from down the street as she ran to catch up with her. "I'm glad I found you."

"Hi, Jessica," Brooke said cheerfully. "I'm a little late. Is Elizabeth here yet?"

"That's why I'm here." Jessica was huffing and puffing. "Elizabeth can't make it. She wanted me to tell you she was sorry. She'll try to call you later."

Brooke looked disappointed. She was holding a notebook and a box of pencils in her hand and had obviously been prepared to start work for the paper right away. "Well," Brooke said, "I guess I'll just stop in and see Julie. Maybe she knows what's up."

Brooke started up the path again.

"No!" Jessica shouted. "I mean, Julie's not here either. They're both gone. They won't be back for a while."

"Hmmm. I wonder if Elizabeth decided to write the article herself," Brooke said. "It *is* a pretty important interview. Oh well, I guess I'll go home."

"I've got a better idea," Jessica said. She knew that Elizabeth was probably on her way to Julie's at this very moment. She had to get Brooke out of sight. "Why don't you come with me? There's something I want to talk to you about."

Brooke hesitated, looking confused. Then she shrugged her shoulders and followed Jessica down the street.

"Where are we going?" she asked Jessica.

Jessica glanced over her shoulder. Luckily, Elizabeth was nowhere in sight. "To the Dairi Burger!" she answered. "Lunch is on me!"

The big grandfather clock in Julie's living room rang once. "It's one o'clock," Julie said, pushing a strand of wavy hair out of her eyes. "Are you sure you told Brooke to meet us at noon?"

"I'm positive," Elizabeth replied. "I can't imagine why she's not here yet. It's not like her. Last night she sounded so excited about working on the paper. Why don't we try her house again," Elizabeth suggested. "Maybe she forgot where we were meeting."

Elizabeth dialed Brooke's number and listened to it ring. There was still no answer.

"She must have forgotten," Julie said after Elizabeth hung up.

"I guess so," Elizabeth replied quietly. But she didn't really believe that Brooke would have forgotten.

"Well," Julie said. "It's lunchtime. Are you hungry?"

"I sure am," Elizabeth said. "Let's go eat."

"Where to?" Jessica asked.

"Where else?" Elizabeth replied as they walked out the front door. "The Dairi Burger!"

Three

◇

"Yum. This pizza burger is great," Lila Fowler said with her mouth full. Jessica, Lila, and Brooke had been joking and laughing and eating for the past half hour.

Brooke took a bite of her own pizza burger and said, "You know, I never thought I could have so much fun with members of the Booster squad." She looked at Jessica and Lila sheepishly. "But I can see I was wrong. You guys are great."

"Well, you may have heard some bad things about us from people who are jealous that they don't fit in," Jessica said.

"As you know," Lila said, "you *do* have to be special to be a Booster."

Jessica smiled at Brooke. Maybe now was the time to bring up the Booster tryouts.

"Did you hear that Tracy Dyer is moving to New York?" Jessica asked.

Brooke nodded vigorously. "I heard! Can you believe it? New York is so far away!"

"Yeah, well, she really left us in a bind," Lila said, glancing at Jessica.

"What do you mean?" Brooke asked.

"Tracy was a member of the Booster squad," Jessica reminded Brooke. "And now we need to fill her spot on the roster."

Brooke looked across the table at Jessica and Lila. "I'm sure you won't have any trouble finding someone," she said. "There are tons of girls in school who would love the chance to try out for the Boosters. I know I would."

Lila sighed. "But that's the problem. We can't take just anyone."

"Lila's right," Jessica said. "The new Booster has to fit in with the rest of us."

"You know," Lila added innocently, "I bet you'd be perfect for that spot."

Brooke blushed a deep red. "Do you really mean it? I don't even know a single cheer," she declared.

"And I've only been to a couple of games all year."

"Don't worry," Lila said reassuringly. "We can teach you the cheers. We just want to make sure we maintain the high standards of the squad."

"It'll be a cinch," Jessica said. "After one afternoon with Lila, you'll know every cheer in our book!"

Jessica shot a quick glance at Lila. She knew the last thing in the world Lila wanted to do was spend an afternoon teaching cheers to Brooke Dennis. But if it meant a chance to meet Kent Kellerman, she knew she would go along with it. "You only need to know two or three cheers for the tryout," Jessica continued. "Then, if you make the squad, you can learn the rest."

Brooke frowned, suddenly remembering she had agreed to do some writing for Elizabeth. "Oh no! I'm not sure I can do it."

"Why not?" Lila asked. "You just said you'd love to try out for the Boosters."

"It's not that I don't want to," Brooke began. "It's just that Elizabeth asked if I wanted to help out on the *Sweet Valley Sixers* and I already told her I would. I'm not sure I'll have time for both." She sighed. "Maybe I should talk to Elizabeth first."

"Oh, I wouldn't worry about that," Jessica told Brooke. "I'll talk to Elizabeth for you. She can get *anyone* to write an article for the paper. It's much harder for us to find exactly the right kind of person to be a Booster."

But Brooke still looked doubtful. "I don't know," she said slowly. "It was so nice of her to offer. It doesn't seem right to just forget about the article."

Jessica tried to think of some way to change Brooke's mind. Maybe talking about the Boosters' upcoming events would help to sway her. "OK, but you don't know what you're missing. We've got a cheerleading competition in Monterey next month."

"It was so much fun last year when we had a full squad," Lila said. "A whole weekend at the beach."

"Plus, in a couple of weeks, we're all going to be modeling for a fashion show at Valley Fashions," Jessica said, keeping an eye on Brooke. "Last time we all got a gift certificate for the store, remember?"

Lila nodded.

"That's really neat," Brooke said. "It sounds like you guys have so much fun."

"Yeah, we're always busy," Lila said.

"But I still don't think I can do it," Brooke said.

Just then, Jessica spotted two girls from her class seated at a booth nearby. "Oh, well," she said, "I guess we'll have to find someone else to try out. Look, Lila. There's Cammi Adams. I bet she'd like to try out for the Boosters." She winked at Lila, hoping she'd play along.

"Oh, sure, Jess," Lila said. "Cammi would be perfect. I saw her in gym class doing gymnastics. She's great at tumbling."

"Let's go talk to her," Jessica said, getting up from the table. "If you change your mind, Brooke, let us know."

"Wait a minute," Brooke said before Jessica and Lila had even left the table. "Maybe you're right. Being on the Boosters does sound like it would be great."

Jessica smiled at Lila as they sat down again. The first part of the plan had worked like a charm.

"I guess I could write an article for the paper some other time," Brooke said.

"Then it's settled," Jessica declared. "Lila will teach you a couple of cheers for the tryout. Of course we can't promise that you'll make the squad," she said. "But I think you've got the best chance."

Elizabeth and Julie rode their bikes into the Dairi Burger parking lot and locked them in the rack near the door.

"Do you see who I see?" Elizabeth said, pointing through the front window of the restaurant.

"Brooke!" Julie exclaimed. "What's she doing with Jessica and Lila?"

Elizabeth shook her head. "I'm not sure," she said, suspecting another one of Jessica's famous schemes. "But I'm going to find out right now."

"Elizabeth! Julie!" Brooke called as soon as the girls entered. "Over here!"

"We've been waiting for you," Elizabeth said as they arrived at the table. "Did you forget about our meeting?" She flashed her twin a suspicious look. "We were starting to get worried," she added.

"Actually," Brooke began, "I was—"

"She was just about to tell you the wonderful news," Jessica interrupted.

Brooke smiled uneasily. "Well, uh, Jessica and Lila have asked me to try out for the Booster squad, and I thought it would be a lot of fun."

"That's great, Brooke," Elizabeth said as she glared at Jessica and Lila. "I'm sure you'd make a wonderful Booster. Can I speak to you for a minute?" Elizabeth said to Jessica through clenched teeth.

Elizabeth led her sister far enough away from the table so no one could hear them. "This had better not have anything to do with meeting Kent Kellerman," she said. "You promised me you wouldn't ask her about it."

"What are you talking about?"

"Brooke was supposed to meet us at Julie's to talk

about the paper and all of a sudden you and Lila are here with her and she's trying out for the Boosters. It sounds suspicious to me, that's all."

"She can try out for anything she wants," Jessica whispered angrily. "Personally, I can't blame her for wanting to try out for the Boosters instead of writing for the paper. It's much more exciting."

Elizabeth glared at her twin. "I don't care if she tries out for the Boosters. Just as long as she's given a fair chance to make it!"

"Don't worry about that," Jessica said before marching back to the table. "She'll get the same chance as anybody else."

"Why don't you and Julie sit down with us," Brooke said when Elizabeth and Jessica returned.

Elizabeth took a seat while Julie went to the counter to order a couple of sodas. She listened while Jessica and Lila made plans to teach Brooke a few of the cheers.

"Elizabeth," Brooke said quietly. "I hope this doesn't cause a problem with the story on Ms. DiNardo."

"Not at all," Elizabeth replied. "I can write the article myself."

"Could I write an article some other time?"

"Sure," Elizabeth said. "We'd love to have you work on the paper."

"Well, enough about that," Jessica said, quickly taking control of the conversation. "Did anyone hear about Kent Kellerman coming to Sweet Valley?"

"I did!" Lila chirped.

"Everybody's heard about it," Julie added, arriving with the sodas. She sat down between Brooke and Elizabeth. "He's going to be filming downtown on Monday."

"I wonder if there's any way we could get to see him?" Jessica asked innocently, staring directly at Brooke.

"I doubt it," Julie said.

"Well, we could just go downtown and watch with the rest of the crowd," Jessica said.

"It's no fun seeing someone like Kent from far away," Lila complained. "I'd rather see him on TV."

Jessica pouted. "I wonder if there's anyone who could help us out." She looked at Brooke again. "I'll bet if we had a couple of passes to the set we could practically touch him!"

"Actually, my father is working on the show," Brooke said. "I'm sure he could get a couple of passes for the set."

Jessica and Lila did their best to act surprised.

Elizabeth couldn't believe it. Jessica was up to her usual tricks. It was just like her to talk Brooke into wanting to join the Boosters just so she could get what she wanted.

"Do you think he would do that for us?" Lila asked, wide-eyed.

"I'm sure he would," Brooke said. "He can get set passes whenever he wants. I've been on lots of sets."

"But they're filming during school hours," Julie reminded everyone.

Brooke shrugged. "My father says these things always take forever. One time he said it took three hours just to film one little scene. I bet they'll be filming all day."

"This is terrific, Brooke. It's definitely the most exciting thing to happen in Sweet Valley in years," Jessica said.

She jumped up from the table when she noticed Elizabeth flashing her a dirty look. She wanted to get out of there before her twin could convince Brooke to change her mind.

"C'mon, Brooke," she said. "Let's go practice some cheers."

Four

◇

"Jessica! Lila! Wait for me!" Brooke called as she rushed down the hallway on Monday morning.

The first bell had already rung and everyone was hurrying to class.

"I need to talk to you," Brooke said as she caught up to them inside the classroom.

"What is it?" Lila asked as she sat down at her usual desk. "Is it about the passes to see Kent?"

"You got them, didn't you?" Jessica demanded.

"They're right here," Brooke said, taking them out

of her bookbag and handing them to Jessica. "But there's a problem," she added sadly.

"What's wrong, Brooke? Can't we get on to the set with these?"

Brooke sighed. "Well . . ." she began.

Suddenly Mrs. Arnette clapped her hands to bring the class to attention. "OK, boys and girls, please stop your talking and place your books under your desks."

The whole class groaned loudly. Mrs. Arnette, whom everyone called "The Hairnet" because she always wore one over her bun, had a fondness for unannounced quizzes. In fact, everyone in school agreed that she was at her most cheerful on the days when she scheduled a surprise quiz.

"I have to talk to you about the passes," Brooke whispered to Jessica.

Jessica placed the set passes inside her social studies book and slid it under her seat. "Tell me after class," she said to Brooke as Mrs. Arnette began to pass out the freshly mimeographed tests.

"Hey, Jessica," Ken Matthews called after her when class had ended and everyone began filing out. "Did you hear about the newest member of your basketball team?"

She hadn't heard anything about a new player.

"What are you talking about, Ken? The season's almost over. We can't have new players on the team. We're playing the championship game on Friday."

"All I know," Ken said, "is I saw her at the playground this weekend and she's one of the best athletes I've ever seen! She was playing softball. She can hit the ball a mile."

Jessica felt a twinge of jealousy. Ever since she had joined the team, Jessica had been considered the best player. Everybody thought so. "What's her name?" she asked, trying to sound uninterested.

"Billie Layton," a voice said.

Jessica turned and came face-to-face with a girl with very short brown hair and dark brown eyes. She was taller than Jessica, and she wore a dark blue frayed sweatshirt, worn white sneakers, and a baseball cap.

"You must be Jessica Wakefield," Billie said with a friendly smile. "I've heard a lot about you already."

Jessica nodded. "I hear you're going to be joining the team this week."

"Yeah," Billie said, thrusting her hands deep into her pockets. "The principal said that since I was playing on the team in my old school, I could finish the season on the team here."

"Well, good luck," Jessica said curtly. "I hope you get a chance to play. We've got some pretty good players already." With that she turned and marched down the hall, Ellen and Lila behind her.

"See you at practice this afternoon," Billie called.

"What a tomboy!" Ellen Riteman said, glancing back to where Billie was standing alone.

"Did you see her clothes?" Lila said. "Looks like she got them at a garage sale!"

"Speaking of garages," Ellen joked, "I heard she refused to take Mrs. Gerhart's cooking class so she could take shop with the boys."

They were all laughing hysterically when Brooke ran up to them.

"Jessica, Lila, I have to talk to you. It's important." She waited for the girls to join her away from the others. "You won't be able to see Kent after school today!"

"Why not?" Lila asked.

Jessica pulled the passes out of her social studies book. "These look OK to me."

"They're fine," Brooke said. "But I found out the whole crew is moving to another location at two o'clock. They'll be gone by the time school is over."

"But I thought you said they'd still be filming after school," Jessica said.

Brooke shook her head. "I'm really sorry, but I was wrong. I know you must be disappointed."

"What time does the filming start?" Jessica asked, still determined to meet Kent.

"It starts at about eleven and goes until about one-thirty," Brooke replied.

Jessica turned to Lila. "That's mostly during lunch and gym class," she said. It was beginning to look hopeless.

"We'll think of something," Lila said as she and Jessica walked away.

As soon as they were sure Brooke couldn't hear them, Lila said, "Brooke doesn't deserve a chance to make the Booster squad. These stupid passes won't do us any good now."

Jessica shrugged her shoulders. "I don't know. Brooke tried her best. She can't help it if Kent won't be there after school."

"You didn't want Brooke to join the Booster squad any more than I did," Lila said, casting an angry look at Jessica. "It's a perfect excuse to eliminate her."

It was true. She really hadn't wanted Brooke to join, but somehow not giving her a chance didn't seem fair. "Come on, Lila. Let's just try to figure out some way to use these passes."

By the time study hall rolled around, they still hadn't come up with a plan.

"Hey, Jess. What's wrong? You look like you just

lost your best friend!" Elizabeth called when she spotted Jessica in the hall. She was on her way to Mr. Bowman's room carrying Caroline Pearce's gossip column for the *Sixers*.

"We're not going to get to see Kent after all," Jessica said glumly. "Brooke got us the passes, but the crew is moving to another location before school lets out."

"Well, maybe you'll see him some other time," Elizabeth consoled.

"Stop the presses!" Caroline Pearce yelled as she ran toward Elizabeth. "The biggest story in Sweet Valley just broke!"

"What is it?" Elizabeth asked. Mr. Bowman didn't like to hold up the printing unless it was really important.

Caroline caught her breath. "There's a new girl in school and Ken Matthews says she's going to star on the basketball, softball, and cross-country teams!"

Jessica huffed loudly. "That's old news, Caroline."

"Everyone in school heard that story before the first bell!" Lila chimed in.

"Ken must have been working overtime to spread the news about Billie Layton," Elizabeth said.

Caroline was fuming. She hated being the last to hear about something. "Well, I'll bet you didn't hear about Ms. Langberg!" she offered.

Suddenly Jessica was all ears. Ms. Langberg was their gym teacher. "What happened to Ms. Langberg?" asked Jessica.

Caroline smiled and paused dramatically. "She got picked for jury duty. She'll be out all this week!"

Jessica and Lila slipped into seats in the back of the room during study hall.

"Hey, Jess," Lila whispered. "Since Ms. Langberg will be gone, why don't we skip gym class today? We can leave at lunchtime and stay all through class. We'd be able to see Kent for sure!"

Jessica shrugged her shoulders. As much as she wanted to meet Kent, she didn't think leaving school would be such a great idea. "What if someone finds out?" she said nervously. "We'd probably get detention for a week, or worse!"

"We won't get caught," Lila insisted.

"But the substitute will know we're not in class when she takes attendance," Jessica reasoned.

Lila thought about it for a moment. "I know!" she said. "We'll get someone to say 'here' for us when our names are called. The substitute doesn't know us. She'll never know the difference."

Jessica remained silent. Lila's plan sounded pretty good, but . . .

"You're not afraid, are you, Jess?" Lila said tauntingly.

"Of course not!" Jessica replied quickly. "It's just . . ."

"If you don't want to go," Lila interrupted, "why don't you give me your pass and I'll go with someone else!"

That did it! It was her idea to get Brooke to give them passes in the first place. Why should Lila act like she was the one in charge? "I'll meet you in the lunch room at eleven-thirty sharp!" Jessica responded curtly. She stood up and gathered her books. "We're going to meet Kent Kellerman after all."

"So, do you want to come along to the shoot?" Jessica asked as she caught up to Elizabeth in the hallway. "We've only got two passes, but I'll bet once we're there they won't even check to see how many we have."

"I thought it was going to be over with before school lets out," Elizabeth said.

"It is, but we're going at lunchtime and staying through gym class."

"Jess, that's playing hooky!" Elizabeth cried.

"Shhh," Jessica hushed. "Don't worry, it's all worked out. Lila has got one of Ellen's friends to say 'here' when our names are called in gym. The substitute will never know the difference."

"Jess," Elizabeth pleaded, "do you know what could happen if you got caught?"

Jessica sighed. "We're not going to get caught, Lizzie. Lila took care of everything. Besides, if I don't go, she's going to think I'm afraid."

Elizabeth shook her head. "You're going to be sorry, Jess," Elizabeth warned her. "Don't expect me to bail you out when you get in trouble."

"Wow, is lunch that bad today?" Amy Sutton asked as she sat down across from Elizabeth in the lunchroom. Amy, Elizabeth's best friend, was a member of the Boosters and a writer for the *Sweet Valley Sixers*. "Looks like you just took a bite of today's mystery meat!"

Elizabeth smiled sadly. "Hi, Amy."

"What's the matter, Liz?"

"Jessica and Lila are cutting class so they can go downtown to see Kent Kellerman," she told Amy. "They'll be in a lot of trouble if they get caught."

"Well, don't worry about them," Amy said. "It's not really your problem."

"I guess you're right," Elizabeth replied. Trying to take her mind off Jessica and Lila, she changed the subject to the next issue of the newspaper.

"I'm thinking of writing an article on the new

girl," Amy said. "She's already got a reputation for being a first-class athlete."

"So I've heard," Elizabeth said. She giggled, recalling how angry Caroline Pearce had gotten earlier. "I thought Caroline was going to hit the ceiling after she found out Ken had beaten her to the scoop!"

Amy nodded, laughing. "I think the queen of gossip is really slipping. She was going around telling everyone that Ms. Langberg had jury duty and wouldn't be in school all week."

Elizabeth froze.

"What's wrong, Liz?" asked Amy.

"How do you know Caroline is wrong about Ms. Langberg?" Elizabeth demanded.

"Because," Amy replied, "I saw Ms. Langberg in the hallway earlier. I even told her about the rumors. She said she had been called for jury duty but was dismissed."

"I can't believe it!" Elizabeth exclaimed. "Jessica and Lila decided to sneak out of Ms. Langberg's class to see Kent Kellerman! They were counting on her being out today. She's sure to miss them if they're not there!"

"Oh no! I didn't know *that* was the class they were skipping. What are you going to do?" Amy asked.

Elizabeth glanced at her watch. There was still

more than half an hour left of lunch. "I'm going to go after them and tell them to come back."

"But what if you don't come back in time?" Amy said. "Then you'll get in trouble, too!"

Elizabeth knew it was true. But she was sure she could make it back in time for class. "I've got to hurry. I'll see you in class." She swept up her books and ran out of the lunchroom as fast as she could.

Five

◇

"Wow! Look at all the people!" Jessica shouted to Lila.

When they arrived downtown, Jessica could hardly believe all the activity going on. There were trucks and trailers parked from one end of the street to the other. It looked as if dozens of crew members carried ladders and lights and cameras. And even though they hadn't seen Kent yet, both girls agreed that this was the most exciting thing to happen in Sweet Valley in a long time.

"C'mon, let's go!" Lila shouted above the noise as she pulled Jessica along by the arm. They quickly made their way through the crowd of enthusiastic fans.

"We've got to find someone to show our passes to," Jessica reminded Lila. Looking around, she spotted an official-looking blond-haired girl holding a clipboard over near the camera. "She must be the one who allows people on the set. Come over this way," Jessica yelled to Lila.

When they reached the girl, Jessica took the two passes from her purse and presented them to her.

"Guests of Mr. Dennis?" the girl asked, scribbling something on her clipboard.

"Yes," Jessica said. She held her breath as the girl looked them over. But after a moment she stepped aside to let them in with no more questions.

"Have fun, and make sure you stay behind the camera."

The two girls let out squeals of excitement as they inched onto the bustling set.

"I've never seen so many people before," Jessica said.

"Who cares about all of them? There's only one person I'm here to see," Lila said.

Suddenly an enormous roar rose from the crowd. Heads turned toward the row of trailers parked along the street. A group of crew members was heading in their direction.

Jessica craned her neck, trying to see what all the commotion was about. Her heart began to pound as the screaming and clapping got louder and louder. Suddenly Jessica could see a familiar-looking person walking onto the set.

"It's him!" Jessica yelled to Lila. "Kent Kellerman!"

Lila stood up on a chair next to Jessica. "I can't believe it," Lila shouted over the roar of the crowd. "He looks even cuter in person than he does on TV!"

Kent made his way through the crowd, smiling and waving to everyone. When he passed Jessica and Lila he smiled directly at them. They yelped with delight.

"He looked right at me!" cried Jessica, dizzy with excitement.

"No, he was staring straight at me!" Lila insisted. "It was obvious!"

But Jessica didn't hear a word Lila had said. She had a dreamy look in her eyes as she stared off at Kent taking his place in front of the camera.

Finally the other actors took their places around Kent. The assistant director picked up a megaphone and turned toward the spectators. "Quiet everyone! Please!" his voice echoed. Soon the crowd had quieted down and the shooting began.

* * *

It took Elizabeth less than ten minutes to get downtown. That left twenty minutes to find Jessica and Lila and make it back to school without getting into trouble. But when she turned the corner and saw the crowd of people in the street she knew it would be nearly impossible.

Dashing into the crowd, Elizabeth glanced around, trying to recall what Jessica had worn to school that day. She remembered her purple blouse and white skirt and scanned the crowd. All the way across the set, she could see Kent talking to the director. And just beyond him, she spotted Jessica and Lila. She pushed her way to the front of the crowd and waved wildly in the direction of the two girls. But their eyes were glued to Kent. "Jessica! Lila!" Elizabeth shouted. "Over here!" But neither of them saw or heard her. And without a pass, Elizabeth couldn't get any closer.

"Please everyone," the assistant director's voice boomed from the megaphone. "Let's have it quiet!"

Elizabeth looked at her watch and sighed. Only ten minutes left. She knew they couldn't get back in time for class to begin, but being late was better than cutting.

She waved her hands and jumped up and down, trying to get Jessica's and Lila's attention.

After what seemed like forever, Lila spotted Elizabeth. Elizabeth saw her poke Jessica in the side and point in her direction.

They both waved to Elizabeth and went back to watching Kent.

They don't understand! Elizabeth realized. What could she do? If she left now, Jessica and Lila would be unaware that Ms. Langberg was in school. Then they'd be caught playing hooky for sure.

But if she stayed, maybe the scene would be over soon and they'd all have a chance to get back before class was over.

When the scene was finally completed, Elizabeth got as close as she could to where Jessica and Lila were standing. "Jessica, Lila, come here!" Elizabeth shouted from behind the barricades.

"What's up, Lizzie?" asked Jessica.

"Yeah, what are you doing here? I thought you didn't care about seeing Kent," Lila said.

"You've got to come back to school right now," Elizabeth said quickly.

"What are you talking about?" Jessica asked.

"Forget it," Lila said. "We want to try to talk to Kent."

Jessica grinned. "He looked right at me, Elizabeth!"

"Ms. Langberg is back at school," Elizabeth said impatiently. "Caroline was wrong!"

"Oh, no!" Jessica cried. "I was afraid something like this might happen! Now we're really in trouble." She looked at Elizabeth. "What are we going to do?"

"We're leaving, that's what we're going to do!" Elizabeth said, leading Jessica away from the set.

Once they made their way through the crowd, the three girls started to run. They didn't have a moment to lose. Elizabeth was going so fast that she nearly tripped. When she steadied herself, she found herself looking straight into a familiar face. It was the principal's secretary, Mrs. Knight, staring right at her!

Lila noticed her, too, as she and Jessica tried to catch up with Elizabeth.

"Oh, no. Do you see who I see?" Lila said, groaning.

Jessica's heart sank when she caught sight of Mrs. Knight through the crowd. "Oh, no! She's going to go right to Mr. Clark. We're in for it now."

The bell rang just as the girls entered the school. Although they had missed gym, they were in time for their next class, math with Ms. Wyler. They ran all the way to the classroom and slipped into their seats.

Julie leaned over and whispered to Elizabeth. "You're in luck," she said. "Ms. Langberg didn't even take attendance. She never knew you were gone!"

Elizabeth groaned to herself. Even though Ms. Langberg didn't notice, Mrs. Knight surely did. She was still in hot water.

Then, just as class was about to begin, Mr. Clark, the principal, knocked on the door. "Ms. Wyler," he said, "I need to see a couple of your students." His eyes wandered over each of them, coming to rest on Jessica and Lila.

"Jessica Wakefield, Lila Fowler," Mr. Clark announced. "Please come with me."

Jessica gulped as she gathered her books and walked to the head of the classroom, followed by Lila.

She cast a gloomy look at Elizabeth just before she marched out of the door.

Elizabeth trembled as she waited for her name to be called. Holding her breath, she watched as Mr. Clark whispered something to Ms. Wyler. Then he strode out of the room without so much as a glance in her direction.

Six

◇

"We're in big trouble," Lila said as they headed toward Mr. Clark's office.

"No kidding!" snapped Jessica. "We'll be lucky if we don't get detention for the rest of the year!"

Lila stopped and stared at Jessica. "He wouldn't do that, would he?"

Jessica shrugged. Anything was possible the way things were going today.

Lila snapped her fingers. "Let's tell him we were on our way to the public library—for some books."

"Forget it, Lila," Jessica said, shaking her head.

"Mr. Clark isn't going to believe any of our stories. Mrs. Knight caught us red-handed."

But what Jessica couldn't understand was why Elizabeth hadn't been called out of class, too. "Mrs. Knight must have seen Elizabeth, too," she said. Then a thought occurred to her. "Unless . . ."

"Unless what?" Lila asked.

"Unless Mrs. Knight thought Elizabeth was me." She looked at Lila. "Mrs. Knight could have seen Elizabeth first," Jessica surmised, "and then thought she was me, knowing that you and I are friends!"

Lila nodded. "You must be right. After all, who would ever think Elizabeth would cut class?"

It was true, Jessica thought. It was natural for Mrs. Knight to think she'd seen her and not Elizabeth.

When they entered the administration office, Mrs. Knight was sitting behind her desk, just outside of Mr. Clark's office.

"In my office, girls," Mr. Clark said as he came through the door behind them.

The girls took seats in front of Mr. Clark's desk.

"First of all," Mr. Clark said grimly, "let me say that I'm very disappointed in both of you." He sat down behind his big wooden desk.

"We're sorry, Mr. Clark," Lila said weakly.

Mr. Clark shook his head slowly. "I'm afraid it's

too late for apologies, girls," he said. "This is very serious."

Jessica and Lila kept their heads lowered.

The principal rose from his chair and came around to the front of the desk. Leaning against the edge, he said, "You're both old enough to know that during the school day we're responsible for you. You are never to leave the school grounds without a teacher's permission." He looked at them for a moment. "Do either of you have anything to say for yourselves?"

Both girls shook their heads.

Mr. Clark folded his arms across his chest. "As punishment, both of you are going to stay after school every day this week."

"Every day?" Lila said.

Jessica thought they were getting off pretty easily.

"And I'm going to call both of your parents," he added. "Skipping classes will not be tolerated."

"Until what time do we have to stay after school, Mr. Clark?" Lila asked.

"Until all the blackboards are washed, of course," he responded. "Make sure you see me first thing after school today, so I can show you where the sponges and wash buckets are kept."

Jessica nodded and slowly got up to leave. She was relieved. She knew it could have been a lot worse.

"Oh, and one last thing," Mr. Clark said. "No extracurricular activities for either of you girls for two weeks," he stated.

Jessica glanced at Lila, horrified.

"That means no dance club, Booster Club, or"—he looked at Jessica—"basketball."

"No basketball!" Jessica moaned. This was the first year the sixth grade had made it to the district championship. It was no secret that Jessica's playing was one of the reasons. And now, just as the big championship game was coming up on Friday, she wasn't allowed to play!

"The entire team—the whole school—is counting on me," she cried to Lila. "If I don't play in Friday's game, everybody in school is going to hate me!"

When Ken Matthews and a few of the other players on the boys' team ran into Jessica later in the day, they gave her the cold shoulder. "Thanks a lot, Jessica!" Ken snapped at her. "Thanks to you, the team just lost its only chance to win the championship."

"But we still have a chance," Jessica said. "Elizabeth is getting pretty good. Don't give up hope yet."

But Ken and his friends just turned and walked away.

All afternoon, everyone treated Jessica as if she had a disease.

After school, Jessica and Lila started making the rounds of the classrooms, scrubbing each blackboard carefully. Lila dunked her sponge into the water bucket and squeezed the water out. "Yuk!" she said. "Do you know what this filthy water must be doing to my hands?" She wiped the blackboard in broad strokes. "Remind me to bring a pair of rubber gloves to school tomorrow."

"Do you know what this is doing to my whole life?" Jessica wailed. "Some girl I've never talked to before in my life called me a traitor! I've never felt so miserable," she complained. "Nobody talks to me, and when they do, they tell me how inconsiderate I am."

Lila groaned and straightened. "I don't know why you didn't tell Mr. Clark that Elizabeth was downtown, too," she said. "It's not fair. She was playing hooky just like us!"

"We can't tell on her," said Jessica.

"Why not?" Lila asked.

"Because we need her."

"We sure could use her help washing the blackboards," Lila said.

Jessica wrung out her sponge and looked at Lila. "No," she said. "We need her for something much more important than that."

*   *   *

"I'm home," Jessica called cheerfully as she walked in the front door late that afternoon. She had kept her fingers crossed the whole way home, hoping that Mr. Clark had forgotten to call. But when she walked into the kitchen, the expression on her mother's face told her otherwise.

Mrs. Wakefield placed her hands on her hips. "What's this about skipping class, young lady?" she said.

Jessica lowered her head. "I guess Mr. Clark called, huh?" she said sheepishly.

"Yes, he certainly did," she replied. "I'm very disappointed in you, Jessica." She shook her head sadly. "Why would you do such a thing?"

Jessica shrugged. "We just wanted to meet Kent so badly, Mom."

"Mr. Clark told me about the punishment he gave you and Lila," Mrs. Wakefield said. "You'll be lucky if your father and I don't find more for you to do."

Jessica looked at her mother, tears welling in her eyes. "Oh, Mom. Washing the blackboards is awful. And we have to skip all our extracurricular activities, too. Isn't that bad enough?"

Mrs. Wakefield walked over to the oven and peered inside. "Your father and I will decide when he gets home," she said sternly.

* * *

"Jessica, can I come in?" Elizabeth poked her head inside her twin's bedroom after dinner that night.

"Sure, come in," Jessica said slowly. Elizabeth entered the room and sat down on Jessica's bed.

"Oh, Jess, I feel so terrible about what happened today. I'm just as guilty as you and Lila. I think I should help with the punishment. Tomorrow I'm going to tell Mr. Clark I missed gym, too."

Jessica jumped up. "Are you crazy?" she shrieked. "If it weren't for you, we would have been in even bigger trouble. You were only trying to help us."

"It's just not right," Elizabeth said. "I did something wrong and I should be punished, too."

"You can't do that!" Jessica said. "You can't forget about the big basketball game."

"What's the championship game have to do with this?" Elizabeth asked.

"If neither of us play in that game, Sweet Valley hasn't got a chance," Jessica pleaded.

Elizabeth sighed heavily. "You know as well as I do, Jess, that there's little chance for us to win if you don't play. You're the whole reason our team is any good."

"That's right," Jessica said. "That's why I have to play!"

"What are you talking about, Jess? You can't play on Friday."

Jessica sat back down beside her sister and flashed her an innocent look. "But it would be so simple, Lizzie. We can switch places, and I'll pretend I'm you for the game on Friday. It's the only chance we have to win the championship."

"No way, Jess!" Elizabeth said, shaking her head vigorously. "You're in too much trouble already."

Jessica had come up with outrageous schemes before, but this one had to be the most incredible. Deceiving the basketball team would be bad enough. But fooling the entire school, well, that was unthinkable.

"C'mon, Lizzie," Jessica pleaded. "No one will know the difference."

But Elizabeth wouldn't give in. "Forget it!" she said, shaking her head. "I already made one big mistake today. I don't intend to make another."

Jessica flopped down on her stomach and sulked. "Oh, Lizzie. My life is ruined! What am I going to do?"

"Look," Elizabeth began quietly, "what would happen if someone found out it was you and not me playing in that game?"

"No one will find out," Jessica said with a sniffle. She brushed her hair away from her face and took the tissue Elizabeth offered her. Then she sat up and looked at her twin with tear-filled eyes. "You can't believe the abuse I got in school today." She blew her nose. "I don't have a single friend left in the whole place! The only time anyone talks to me is to tell me what a creep I am!" She tumbled back onto the bed, sobbing.

"C'mon, Jess," Elizabeth said. "In a few days everyone will forget what happened. Who knows, maybe we'll win the game anyway. I'm getting pretty good. You said so yourself."

Jessica's tears flowed even harder. She buried her face in the pillow. "You're the only one who can save me!" she sobbed.

Elizabeth sat down on the bed beside Jessica. As usual, she found her twin impossible to resist. "I have a feeling I'm making the biggest mistake of my life," Elizabeth said, relenting. "But I'll do it."

Jessica sat up and hugged her sister as hard as she could. A bright smile flashed across her tear-stained face almost immediately.

"Oh, Lizzie, you're the greatest sister in the whole wide world!" she cried. "Thanks to you, the sixth grade is going to win that game on Friday!" She gave Elizabeth one last giant hug. "You won't regret this!"

Elizabeth hoped her sister was right.

Seven

◇

"Don't forget, Lizzie, we've got to switch clothes right after school today," Jessica called from the bathroom at a quarter to eight on Tuesday morning.

Elizabeth was already dressed and ready to go. Jessica, late as usual, was standing in front of the full-length mirror in her room hastily tying a purple ribbon around her ponytail.

Elizabeth dropped her bookbag on her bed and barged into her sister's room. "What are you talking about?" she asked. "I agreed to switch places with you for *one* day—Friday, the day of the game."

"But what about practice?" Jessica said innocently.

Elizabeth couldn't believe her ears. "What's practice got to do with this?"

"Oh, Lizzie, you've just got to do me this one last favor," Jessica said. "If I don't practice this week I won't have a chance at leading the team to victory."

Elizabeth stood with her hands on her hips. It was no use. She had agreed to let Jessica play in the game in her place on Friday, and now she'd have to go along with the rest of the plan.

When they arrived at school that morning, Elizabeth got an idea of what Jessica was going through at school. Almost no one talked to her.

"You see?" Jessica complained to Elizabeth as three girls from the Booster squad walked past without saying hello. "It's as if I don't exist."

"I'm sure if you went over to them they'd talk to you," Elizabeth said. "Besides, can you blame them? If you hadn't skipped school, none of this would have happened."

Jessica shook her head in disbelief. "So now you're against me, too," she said. "That's just great."

"Oh, Jess. I am not. Hey, look. I bet Ellen Riteman and Tamara Chase, your fellow Unicorns, are still talking to you."

"I don't know," Jessica said as Elizabeth grabbed her by the arm and dragged her over to the two girls, who were huddled together looking at a sheet of paper.

"Hey, what's going on?" Jessica asked.

Tamara handed the sheet of paper to Jessica. It was the sign-up sheet for the Booster tryouts that were to take place that afternoon. Neither girl looked too happy.

"Some choices," Tamara said sarcastically.

"It's not going to be easy to find someone from this list," Ellen said.

Jessica looked it over and nodded. "You're right. Only a couple of these girls even come close to being Booster squad material." She showed the list to Elizabeth. "I guess Brooke really wasn't as interested in the Boosters as we thought. She didn't even sign up."

Elizabeth searched the list for Brooke's name, but it wasn't there. Brooke had seemed so excited about joining the Boosters the other day. Elizabeth handed the list back to Tamara. "Did Brooke see the sign-up sheet?"

"Of course," said Tamara. "She told me she thought it over and decided not to try out. It's too bad," she added. "She might have been our first choice."

"Well, I'm going to find her," Elizabeth said as she left the group. She knew Brooke had history during first period. As she ran down the hall, she spotted Amy Sutton on her way to class. "Amy, come with me," she said. They reached Mrs. Arnette's classroom just as Brooke was about to enter.

"I saw the sign-up sheet for the Booster tryouts," Elizabeth said to Brooke. "There seemed to be one name that was missing."

Brooke shrugged. "I'm not going to try out," she said. "I've been trying to practice the cheers, but I can't do them. And Lila doesn't seem to want to help me."

"Did she say she wouldn't?" Amy asked angrily.

"Well, no," Brooke admitted. "But I think the only reason they even asked me to try out for the squad was so I would get them those passes to see Kent." She shook her head. "I guess I was pretty dumb to think they'd really want me to join, huh?"

"No, not at all, Brooke," Elizabeth said, trying to hide her anger. "I don't think you should give up now."

"That's the way the Boosters are sometimes," Amy said. "They think they can get away with anything because they're popular."

"Amy, would you be willing to teach Brooke a few cheers?" Elizabeth said, suddenly getting an idea. "I know a way for us to get back at Jessica and Lila."

"How?" Brooke asked.

"If you're the best of those trying out, they'll have no choice but to pick you," Elizabeth said. "Will you help her, Amy?"

"Of course," Amy said. "I'd love to. They treated me the same way when I was first trying out for the squad. I know what you're going through, Brooke."

"Would you really help me?" Brooke asked.

"Sure," Amy said. "I'll bet after one more practice session, you'll have the cheers down pat. Meet me right outside the gym after school."

"I'll be there," Brooke said as the bell for first period rang and the girls hurried off to their classes.

When the last class of the day had ended, Jessica ran through the halls searching frantically for Elizabeth. Basketball practice began right after school. There wasn't a moment to waste.

"Elizabeth!" Jessica called as she spotted her sister at the end of the hall. She pointed to the bathroom door, then slipped inside and waited for Elizabeth.

"I'm not sure about this," Elizabeth complained as she burst through the door after Jessica. "It's been bothering me all day. I don't see why we can't just do this on Friday."

Jessica stared at Elizabeth and frowned. "I thought we already decided," she said. She untied the purple ribbon from her ponytail and handed it to Elizabeth.

"There isn't time to change all our clothes. Just put your hair in a ponytail and tie this around it."

Before Elizabeth could say another word, Jessica had bolted through the door and was gone.

Tying the ribbon in her hair, Elizabeth was afraid she had gotten herself into a real mess. How was she supposed to have time for any of her own activities if she had to stay after school every day? She had a lot of work to do for the paper, for one thing. On no! The paper . . . How could she have forgotten? Today was the interview with Ms. DiNardo!

Elizabeth looked at her watch and gasped. The interview was supposed to take place at Madame André's dance studio in just fifteen minutes. If she hurried, she could still make it. She had to tell Jessica that the plan was off for today. Jessica would be angry, but there was no way around it.

Elizabeth burst through the door into the hallway. She prayed that she would catch up to Jessica before she made it to the locker room. But as she rounded the corner just a few feet from the gym, she slid to a stop.

Standing before her was Mr. Clark.

"Jessica!" he said, smiling. "I've been looking all over for you."

Elizabeth's heart sank. She suddenly remembered the purple ribbon she'd tied in her hair.

Mr. Clark took Elizabeth by the arm and led her down the hall.

"I'm sorry, Mr. Clark," Elizabeth pleaded. "I can't clean the blackboards today! I have to go somewhere! It's very important!"

"Is it a doctor's appointment?" Mr. Clark asked.

Elizabeth didn't know what to say. If she told Mr. Clark she wasn't Jessica, it might ruin the plan for Friday. And she couldn't lie. He would surely ask for a note from the doctor. Instead she just shook her head sadly.

"I thought so," Mr. Clark said knowingly. "Now, if you'll come with me, I'm sure Lila will be happy to know she won't be all by herself today."

Eight

◇

Jessica bounced the basketball nervously as she watched Billie Layton take a shot at the far end of the court. The ball swished through the hoop cleanly.

Billie really was as good as Ken and Caroline had been saying.

"She's really great," Sarah Thomas said to Jessica. Sarah was one of the team's best reserves. "She may be just what we need for Friday's game. Don't you think, Elizabeth?"

"Oh, she's pretty good," Jessica said, pretending to be Elizabeth. "It's too bad Jessica isn't here. I'm sure she'd show Billie Layton a thing or two about basketball."

"Oh, I don't know," Sarah said, shaking her head. "Everyone thinks Billie's even better than Jessica."

Jessica bit her tongue. Billie was good, there was no doubt about it. But Jessica was sure she was better.

"Anyway, I know she's your sister and all," Sarah went on, "but I think it was pretty selfish of Jessica to play hooky. She should be thankful that Billie came along when she did. Now at least we still have a chance at winning."

Jessica was just about to give Sarah a piece of her mind when the coach, Ms. Langberg, called Elizabeth's name to take Nora Mercandy's place. Trotting out onto the court, Jessica vowed that on Friday she would prove she was the best player in Sweet Valley. Even if everyone was going to think it was Elizabeth!

"This is the most cruel and unusual punishment ever!" Lila complained loudly. Her voice echoed down the empty hall as she and Elizabeth walked wearily toward the next classroom with their buckets of water.

Elizabeth was hardly listening. She was thinking about how angry Madame André was going to be when she found out that she had missed the interview with Ms. DiNardo.

She was just about to enter the room when she spotted Mr. Bowman at the end of the hall. "Oh, no," she said under her breath.

"Jessica!" Mr. Bowman called. "I need to speak to you."

Elizabeth waited nervously as Mr. Bowman came down the hallway quickly. "Have you seen Elizabeth?" he asked. "She was supposed to do a very important interview today and I just got a call that she hasn't shown up yet. I'm worried about her."

Elizabeth's heart was pounding. What could she do? "Um, Elizabeth?" she stammered. "Actually Mr. Bowman, I'm—"

"I saw Elizabeth!" Lila exclaimed suddenly. "She's in the gym. Practicing with the basketball team."

"Practicing?" Mr. Bowman said, relieved. "I was afraid something had happened to her. She was supposed to interview Ms. DiNardo at three-thirty."

"Maybe the interview can be rescheduled for later this afternoon," Elizabeth said hopefully. "Elizabeth probably couldn't leave practice since I'm not there to play. I'm sure she'll be happy to do the interview afterward, though."

"Hmmm. I'm surprised at her," Mr. Bowman said. "Ms. DiNardo is a very important person, and it's not like Elizabeth to keep anyone waiting."

"Don't be too hard on her," Elizabeth pleaded.

"I'm sure she's got an explanation." She hoped Mr. Bowman wouldn't be too angry.

"That's exactly what I'm about to find out," Mr. Bowman said as he turned on his heel and headed for the gym.

Elizabeth only hoped Jessica would come up with a good explanation.

Ms. Langberg blew her whistle and called Jessica over to the sidelines.

"Mr. Bowman would like to speak to you, Elizabeth," Ms. Langberg said. She motioned for Billie Layton to take her place in the lineup.

Mr. Bowman stared at Jessica. "Elizabeth, what happened? Did you forget about the interview with Ms. DiNardo?"

Jessica had no idea who Ms. DiNardo was. "Uh, Ms. DiNardo?" she repeated.

"She was waiting for you at the ballet school for almost half an hour," Mr. Bowman said. "I'm surprised at you, Elizabeth."

Jessica shifted from foot to foot. She wanted to get back out on the court. "I'm sorry, Mr. Bowman. I couldn't get out of practice today. Is there any way to reschedule the interview?"

"It's already been done," he replied. "But you're going to have to leave practice a little early today."

"But I can't!" Jessica cried. "If I leave, we'll be short a player." She turned quickly as the crowd behind her cheered another sparkling play by Billie.

"I'm afraid there's no other way," Mr. Bowman explained. "Ms. DiNardo will be at her hotel downtown at four. She said she can do the interview then." He looked at his watch. "You should leave in a few minutes," he added. "Don't be late!"

Jessica had to think of something fast! She didn't know the first thing about doing an interview. But if someone didn't talk to Ms. DiNardo at four, Elizabeth would be in trouble. And that would mean trouble for Jessica.

Looking out across the gymnasium, Jessica saw the Booster squad tryouts being held in the corner. She noticed Brooke Dennis standing in line waiting to try out, and she suddenly had a great idea.

She dashed across the gym just as Brooke was about to perform a cheer.

"Wait!" Jessica shouted. "I need to talk to you, Brooke." She pulled Brooke aside. "I thought you decided not to try out for the Boosters. What are you doing here?"

Brooke looked confused. "Don't you remember? Amy and I practiced some cheers right after school. From the look of things I've got a pretty good chance to make the squad."

"Well," Jessica began, "remember that interview I asked you to do?"

Brooke nodded. "Of course. The one with Ms. DiNardo."

"Exactly!" said Jessica. "Since Jessica is out, I really need to be here at practice. And the interview's at four. Would you still like to—"

"You want me to do the interview!" Brooke broke in happily. "After I backed out once before! Of course I'll do it!" She turned to explain to the Boosters, "Elizabeth really needs me to do this interview. Do you think I could try out next time?"

They all shook their heads. No one looked pleased. "Sorry, Brooke," Janet Howell said. "If you want to try out, you'll have to do it now. We have to make a decision right away."

Brooke looked at Jessica, then quickly back to them. "Then I won't try out," she said. "This is more important. Come on, Elizabeth."

The two girls walked away from the Booster try-outs.

"What do I have to do?" Brooke asked Jessica. "I don't even know the first thing about interviewing."

"Um, well, bring a notebook and a pencil," Jessica began. "And remember, Ms. DiNardo is a star, so ask her about the other famous people she's met. Celebrities like to talk about that kind of thing."

"Thanks, Elizabeth," Brooke said. "I'm really excited about this. I wanted to be a Booster, but if I can't do both, then I think I'd rather write for the *Sweet Valley Sixers*. Anyway, I feel pretty badly about the way Jessica and Lila treated me."

"Well, you'd better hurry," Jessica said, biting her lip. "We can't keep Ms. DiNardo waiting any longer."

"Where do I go?" asked Brooke.

"Madame André's dance studio," answered Jessica.

"Oh, and by the way," Brooke added, "you're invited to my house for dinner on Thursday. My father is having some people over from work. One of the guests is bringing the greatest apple pie in the world!"

"That sounds like fun," Jessica said. "I'll be there."

"Great!" said Brooke. "Well, I'd better hurry if I want to make it to the ballet school by four. Wish me luck!"

Jessica smiled to herself as she headed back over to basketball practice. She hoped Elizabeth appreciated her quick thinking. If it weren't for her, Elizabeth would be in a heap of trouble!

It was almost dark by the time Elizabeth walked through the back door into the kitchen. Jessica was busy peeling potatoes while her mother seasoned a roast.

"How was basketball practice, dear?" Mrs. Wakefield asked Elizabeth.

"Okay," Elizabeth said weakly. She was exhausted.

"Keeping you there pretty late, huh?" Steven said, popping a Fig Newton into his mouth. "I guess you girls must need a lot of practice since you lost your big gun."

Jessica smiled at her twin.

Elizabeth just groaned. Her back was sore from washing blackboards, and she didn't feel like talking one bit. "Call me when dinner is ready," she said, trudging out of the room and up the stairs.

She was just beginning to doze off when she heard a knock on her door.

Jessica opened the door slowly. "Lizzie, it's me. Don't you want to hear how I handled Mr. Bowman today?" she asked proudly. "I was brilliant."

"Actually, I was afraid to ask," muttered Elizabeth. "But go ahead."

By the time Jessica had finished telling her about Brooke, Elizabeth was sitting up on her bed grinning.

"You were right!" Elizabeth exclaimed. "You were

fabulous! I thought I was in trouble for sure, but you really came through for me this time."

"See?" Jessica said proudly. "With me at the controls, you have nothing to worry about. I even remembered to tell you that Brooke has invited you to dinner Thursday night."

Elizabeth dashed into the hallway. "Thanks. I'll bet Brooke is just dying to tell me all about the interview," she squealed. She picked up the phone and dialed. "I can't wait to hear all about it!"

Nine

◇

"Hurry up! We'll be late for school!" Elizabeth called up to Jessica the next morning.

She grabbed her bookbag from the kitchen table and headed for the door, anxious to get to school. She had tried calling Brooke all night but there had been no answer. She was dying to hear about the interview with Ms. DiNardo.

"I'm coming!" Jessica called from the landing. She pulled her favorite purple sweater over her head and hurried down the stairs.

"How are things at school these days, Jess?" Elizabeth teased as they walked to school. "Are you still at the bottom of the social ladder?"

"Very funny," Jessica said dryly. "For your information, school is horrible. All I keep hearing about is how Billie Layton is going to save the day. I can't wait till the game on Friday. I plan to show everyone in that school that I'm the best player in Sweet Valley."

Elizabeth shook her head. "Jess, even if you win the game single-handedly, everyone is going to think you're me!"

"At least they won't say Billie Layton was the star!" Jessica said.

Elizabeth laughed. Leave it to Jessica to come up with her very own logic.

When they arrived at school, Brooke was waiting for Elizabeth outside.

"Hi, Brooke," Elizabeth said. "How did it go yesterday? I'll bet Ms. DiNardo is fascinating!"

"I've got some bad news, Elizabeth," Brooke mumbled nervously. "I don't know where to begin. After I left here yesterday, I ran all the way to the ballet school, but when I got there Madame André and Ms. DiNardo were gone." She looked as though she might cry. "I didn't do the interview."

"What do you think happened?" Elizabeth asked as the girls climbed the final steps.

"I don't know. The school was closed when I got

there," Brooke said. "I called your house right away, but no one was home. I even ran back here, but you were gone. By then it was late and I had to meet my father at a restaurant."

"Don't worry, Brooke," Elizabeth said reassuringly. "Let's go talk to Mr. Bowman. Maybe he knows what happened."

When they reached Mr. Bowman's classroom, Elizabeth never had a chance to ask him anything.

"Good morning, girls. Elizabeth, would you like to tell me what happened? Ms. DiNardo called this morning to tell me that you never showed up yesterday."

"It was all my fault," Brooke blurted out. "Elizabeth asked me to do the interview in her place. But when I got to the ballet school, no one was there." Brooke looked at the floor. "I guess it took me too long to get there."

"You went to the ballet school?" Mr. Bowman asked Brooke.

"Yes," she replied. "I even ran back here afterward to see if there was a change in plans, but everyone was gone."

"Elizabeth, I told you that Ms. DiNardo was at her hotel. It's not like you to forget something so important."

Elizabeth couldn't believe it. She should have

known that Jessica wouldn't get the information straight.

"I'm sorry, Mr. Bowman," Elizabeth pleaded. "I guess I just got confused. Please just give us one more chance. I promise this time we'll get the interview."

Mr. Bowman shook his head. "I'm afraid I can't give you another chance. Ms. DiNardo left for San Diego this morning after she called me. Today is Wednesday. You have until Friday to have another article for me in place of the interview."

Elizabeth and Brooke walked out of the classroom in silence. Where were they going to get a story so quickly?

"I'm sorry," Brooke frowned. "I really messed up this time, didn't I?"

"Of course not," Elizabeth said. "It wasn't your fault at all. I forgot to tell you to go to the hotel."

"I should have been more careful," Brooke grumbled. "You were so busy with the basketball team. I should have double-checked everything."

Elizabeth patted Brooke on the back. "Don't you worry," she said. "We'll think of another story."

Brooke smiled. "You're right," she said firmly. "We've got today and tomorrow to come up with something. If we put our heads together, I'm sure we can do it."

*   *   *

Later that morning, Elizabeth caught up with Jessica as she was leaving study hall. Jessica took one look at Elizabeth and knew she was in trouble.

"Jessica!" Elizabeth whispered angrily. "You really did it this time."

"What did I do?" Jessica asked.

Elizabeth took a deep breath. "You sent Brooke on a wild goose chase, that's what you did. You sent her to Madame André's school instead of to the hotel where Ms. DiNardo was waiting."

"I'm sorry, Lizzie," she said innocently. "But I was thinking about so many things when Mr. Bowman talked to me. I thought he said Ms. DiNardo would be at the school. And anyway, what's the big deal? Can't you just interview her today instead?"

"No!" Elizabeth shot back. "She's gone!"

"Why don't you write a story about something else?"

"Thanks to you that *is* what I have to do!" Elizabeth snapped. "And on top of that, it has to be finished by Friday morning."

"Lizzie, I'm sorry," Jessica said soothingly. "Don't be angry at me. I couldn't stand it if you were. Without you I'd go through school every day without having anyone to talk to." She flashed a smile at Elizabeth, hoping to see one in return. "You're my only friend in the world."

"*Was* your only friend in the world," Elizabeth cried. "You'll be lucky if I ever speak to you again!"

For the rest of the day, Elizabeth tried to think of a new story. She met with Brooke during study hall, and together they tried to come up with new ideas. Later they met at the library.

"How about a story on the new girl, Billie Layton?" Brooke suggested. "I hear she's a big hit with the basketball team."

Elizabeth shook her head. "Amy's already doing one. We could ask Julie Porter's dad if he would agree to be interviewed," she added. "He's a conductor with a big orchestra. He was on TV once."

Brooke nodded. "That's a good idea. I'm sure he's got lots of interesting stories."

Elizabeth jotted Mr. Porter's name down in her notebook.

"How about Nora Mercandy's grandfather?" Brooke offered. "Someone told me he was a world-famous magician."

"Marvelous Marvin!" Elizabeth said. She remembered how foolish everyone had felt when they discovered Mr. Mercandy was the victim of a stroke and not a zombie as they'd thought. "He even knew Houdini!" she said, scribbling his name down.

"Any other local celebrities?" Brooke wondered out loud.

"Amy Sutton's mother is a reporter for KSV-TV!" Elizabeth recalled. "Do you think she'd let us interview her?"

"It can't hurt to ask," Brooke said.

Elizabeth shut her notebook and gathered her things together. "I'll call these people tonight. Surely one of them has the time to answer a few questions for the paper."

"Call me tonight," Brooke said.

But when Elizabeth finally called Brooke late that night, she had bad news.

"Mrs. Sutton and Mr. Porter are both working out of town," she told Brooke. "And Mr. Mercandy's wife said he wasn't feeling well. It looks like it's back to the drawing board."

"There must be *someone* in Sweet Valley we can interview," Brooke said.

"What about your father?" Elizabeth suggested. "I can't believe we forgot him. He's a celebrity."

Brooke laughed. "It's hard to think of my father as a celebrity," she said. "Anyway, he's away until tomorrow night. Remember? You're having dinner with us. We'd better think of someone else."

"OK." Elizabeth sighed. "But something tells me it isn't going to be easy."

By the time Elizabeth arrived home from school on Thursday, she was about ready to give up.

"Hi, Lizzie!" Jessica called as Elizabeth walked through the door and dropped her bookbag on the floor. "How was basketball practice?" she asked with a wink.

Elizabeth didn't even look at her sister.

Mr. Wakefield came over and gave his elder daughter a hug. "Looks like they're drilling you pretty hard for that big game. How are things at school?"

"Not too good," Elizabeth answered. "Brooke Dennis and I are supposed to write an article about someone, only we can't find anybody to interview."

"Why don't you interview Steven," Jessica suggested. "He's the human vacuum cleaner!"

"Thanks, Jess. You're a big help. Oh, Mom. I forgot to tell you. Brooke invited me to have dinner at her house tonight."

"It doesn't look like you have much energy for dinner, much less a trip to Brooke's," Mrs. Wakefield said. "Are you sure you want to go?"

Elizabeth shrugged wearily. "Maybe you're right," she said. "I think I'll go wash up, then call Brooke and cancel."

When the phone in the Wakefield kitchen rang, Jessica jumped up to answer it. "Hello," she said. When she heard the voice on the other end of the line, she rolled her eyes. "Elizabeth," she called toward the bathroom. "It's for you."

Jessica handed the phone to Elizabeth and made a face. "It's Brooke," she said.

Elizabeth took the phone from Jessica. "Hi, Brooke. I was just about to call you," she said. "I'm pretty tired. I don't think I'm going to be able to make dinner."

"Are you sure about that?" Brooke said. Elizabeth noticed a hint of excitement in her voice.

"I'm sorry, Brooke," Elizabeth said. "Maybe some other time."

"Well, OK," Brooke sighed. "But I sure could use some help with an interview I'm going to do."

"You found someone to interview?" Elizabeth asked.

When Brooke told Elizabeth who was going to be at her house, Elizabeth cried out happily. She hung up the phone and started jumping up and down. When she calmed down, she told her mother she had decided to go to Brooke's house after all.

"You're not going to believe this, Jess!" she said, turning to face her sister. "Kent Kellerman is going to be at Brooke's house!"

Jessica's mouth dropped open a mile.

"That's wonderful, dear," Mrs. Wakefield said.

"And Brooke's father said Kent wouldn't mind answering a few questions! This could be the best interview we've ever had in the paper. I'd better go get ready."

Jessica looked longingly after her twin. "Do you think Brooke would mind if I went along, too, Mom?" she asked. "I want to meet Kent!"

"I don't know whether Brooke would mind," Mr. Wakefield said in a no-nonsense tone. "But I sure would. You've been grounded, young lady, remember?"

Ten

◇

"Kent said Sweet Valley was one of the nicest places he'd ever visited," Elizabeth said as she and Jessica walked to school the next morning. "He said he might even want to move here one day."

Jessica looked at her twin. "What was that, Liz?" she said. "I'm sorry. I wasn't listening."

Jessica had been pretending all morning that meeting Kent Kellerman wasn't such a big deal.

"I said Kent told me he can't wait to meet the younger twin of the Wakefield clan," Elizabeth joked.

"Are you kidding?" Jessica yelped. "Did he ask about me?"

Elizabeth reached into her bookbag and handed Jessica a big envelope. "Open it," she said.

Jessica quickly tore it open and pulled out a full-color photo of Kent. "To Jessica. All my love, Kent," she read aloud. "Did he really write this?"

"Of course."

Jessica hugged the picture to her chest and sighed. "I can't wait for everyone at school to see this! How did the interview come out?"

"Great," Elizabeth said. "I got up extra early to type it up." She couldn't wait to show it to Mr. Bowman.

"So when do I get to read it?" Jessica wanted to know. "Don't I get first crack at it? After all, my own sister wrote it."

"Your sister *and* Brooke Dennis," corrected Elizabeth. "You can read it when it comes out in the paper. I have to turn it in right away."

When Elizabeth got to school, she found Brooke, and the two of them walked to Mr. Bowman's room to hand in the article. They had a hard time containing their excitement. When Mr. Bowman saw whom they had interviewed, even he couldn't hide his pleasure.

"This is wonderful, girls," he said, glancing

through the story. "I'll admit, I didn't think you were going to make the deadline. I'm very glad you did."

"We also wrote these," said Elizabeth, handing him two envelopes. "Apologies to Madame André and Ms. DiNardo."

"We're really sorry, Mr. Bowman," Brooke added.

"I'll make sure they get these," he said, placing the envelopes in his briefcase.

"This story may double our circulation," Elizabeth told Brooke when they left Mr. Bowman's room.

"That was the most fun I've had in a long time," Brooke said, beaming. "It will be so exciting to see my name in the paper."

Elizabeth smiled. "On the front page, too! It looks like things turned out better than we expected."

Brooke laughed. "I'll say! And guess what. Janet Howell called my house last night after you left. She offered to give me a special tryout during lunch today. I guess they didn't find anyone else good enough for the squad."

"That's wonderful, Brooke," Elizabeth said. "Are you going to try out? I'm sure you would make it."

"Well, I don't know," Brooke said. "I was kind of hoping to write another story for the paper."

"I've got just the assignment for you," Elizabeth said. "How about covering this afternoon's championship game?"

"I'd love to," said Brooke. "It'll give me a chance to write a story on my own. And who knows, if you make the winning shot, it might be about you."

Elizabeth nodded but didn't say anything. She still hated the idea of lying about playing in the game this afternoon. She couldn't wait for this week to be over. "I guess I'll see you at the game," she said as she and Brooke parted.

After school, Jessica sat on a bench in the locker room nervously lacing up her sneakers. After a short pep talk from Ms. Langberg, the team ran out onto the court to warm up amid wild cheers.

"I've never seen this gym so crowded," Jessica said to Nora Mercandy.

"I just hope they all go home happy," Nora said. "We've just got to win."

When the game was about to begin, Jessica stood up to take her place with the other players. But when Ms. Langberg came over and tapped her on the shoulder, she knew something was wrong. "Elizabeth, Billie Layton is going to start today," she said. "With Jessica out, she's the best starting player."

Jessica was stunned. All week long she had waited for this moment, and now she was being taken out before the game even began. "But Ms. Langberg,"

Jessica pouted, "I've been practicing so hard this week. I just know I'll do great."

"I'm sorry, Elizabeth," she replied. "But don't worry, you'll have a chance to play, too."

Jessica sat down on the end of the bench and watched nervously as the opponents quickly reached a 10–0 lead.

Jessica fretted. She turned to Sarah Thomas. "We're going to lose," she said mournfully. "I just know it."

"We can still win," Sarah replied.

But Jessica could tell that even Sarah didn't quite believe it.

After the first few minutes, the Sweet Valley team began to score some points. "Let's go, Sweet Valley!" Jessica yelled, jumping out of her seat. The rest of the team on the bench started to cheer along with her.

In no time, Sweet Valley had cut the lead to 10–6 on a jump shot by Billie from fifteen feet. Jessica stood up and cheered. She wanted to get into the game more than anything. *I can win this game for us*, she said to herself. *I just know it!*

With just a few minutes left in the second quarter, Jessica was beginning to wonder if she would ever play. Sweet Valley had fought back to within two points, and the other team seemed to be getting tired.

"Elizabeth!" Ms. Langberg called to Jessica. "You're in for Billie."

Jessica quickly removed her warm-up suit and took her place with her teammates on the court. But suddenly the other team rattled off six quick points, and it looked as if they were going to run away with the game again. Jessica could see people in the stands getting up to leave.

"There goes our only chance," she heard Ken Matthews say during a time-out. Jessica glanced up at the scoreboard. The opponents were leading by ten points again. It was beginning to look hopeless.

When Jessica saw Ken and his friends heading for the exits, she knew she had to do something fast. *If we lose this game, they'll blame it all on me*, she thought.

As the other team came down the court, Jessica stole a pass and drove the length of the court for an easy lay-up. A few people in the crowd stopped on their way out and watched as Jessica grabbed a rebound and made a perfect pass to Nora for an easy two points.

The crowd roared.

The next time Jessica looked at the scoreboard, Sweet Valley Sixth was back in the game. The score was tied. She also saw the stands were filled again with excited spectators. No one was going to leave now.

"You're playing great," Billie said to Jessica just before the start of the second half. "Keep it up."

Jessica nodded.

"Hey, Elizabeth," Nora said. "Jessica must have taught you a few tricks. You look like a pro."

"Don't let us down now, Elizabeth," Ken Matthews shouted from the stands.

Jessica waved to Ken, beaming proudly. As soon as the game resumed, she picked up right where she had left off in the first half. She made her first three shots in a row, and Sweet Valley had the lead for the first time since the game began. They held on to their lead through the last quarter, and when the final buzzer went off, the whole team lifted Jessica onto their shoulders and carried her off the court chanting, "Hooray for Liz!"

After the crowd quieted down, Ms. Langberg took her place behind the podium in the gym. "Quiet, everyone," she said into the microphone. "It's time to announce the Most Valuable Player award."

As the gym buzzed with excitement, the whole team circled around Jessica, smiling. No one had a doubt as to who would win it.

"The winner is Elizabeth Wakefield," Ms. Langberg announced.

The crowd shouted their approval as they stood on their feet and applauded.

Jessica walked up to the podium grinning from ear to ear.

Ms. Langberg handed Jessica the big trophy. Jessica grabbed it and hoisted it high above her head for all to see. "Thank you, everyone," she said into the microphone. "This is the happiest moment in my life. I knew we would win if I played." She suddenly realized she didn't sound at all like her sister. "At least I thought I could help the team win if I got the chance," she added modestly.

Ms. Langberg congratulated Jessica again as she stepped up to the mike. "Elizabeth's name will be engraved on the front of the trophy," she said. "Let's all give her one last cheer!"

The crowd roared.

By the time Jessica got home, she was exhausted. Not only did her face hurt from smiling so much, her mind was racing from having to remember to act as unassuming as Elizabeth. It wasn't easy. It only proved to Jessica that Elizabeth needed to be taught how to enjoy herself more.

But Jessica went to sleep without a worry on her mind. There was no doubt about it. Winning the game had been the most incredible experience of her life.

Eleven

◇

"I'll get it!" Elizabeth heard Steven shout as the phone rang. It was Saturday morning and the phone had been ringing nonstop since nine o'clock. Elizabeth thought the whole school was going to call before noon.

"Elizabeth," Steven shouted up the stairs. "It's someone named Billie Layton."

Elizabeth picked up the phone in the upstairs hall. "Hi, Billie," she said. "It was really an exciting game yesterday, wasn't it?"

"It sure was," Billie said. "I just called to tell you

what a great game you played. You were terrific."

"Thanks, Billie," Elizabeth replied modestly. "From what I heard . . . I mean . . . I thought you could have easily been picked for MVP instead of me."

"I don't think so," Billie said. "The way you were playing yesterday, no one could have matched you. It was really exciting to watch you play."

Elizabeth didn't know what to say. Everyone was calling to congratulate her this morning. It was really beginning to bother her.

"Why don't we play some one-on-one next week?" Billie said.

"I'd love to," Elizabeth said. "I'll see you in school on Monday."

After Elizabeth hung up, she went out back and climbed onto the low branch of a tree that served as her thinking seat. She didn't want to get any more calls from friends congratulating her. It wasn't really the basketball game that was bothering her. It was skipping her class that had been gnawing at her all week. From the very beginning, she had wanted to tell her parents the truth: that she had been downtown chasing after Jessica and Lila. But Jessica had talked her out of it. Now, after it was all over, Elizabeth thought about it again and realized she had to tell them what really happened.

Mr. Wakefield was out back skimming the pool when Elizabeth crawled out from under the tree and walked over to him. "I have something I need to talk to you and Mom about," she said.

"Hmmm, sounds serious," Mr. Wakefield said. He stopped what he was doing and followed Elizabeth into the house.

"It's about playing hooky," Elizabeth said when her mother and father were seated around the kitchen table. She went on to tell them everything that had happened on Monday, including how Mrs. Knight must have mistaken her for Jessica.

"I was trying to save Jessica from getting into trouble. Instead I made things worse," Elizabeth said, lowering her head.

Mr. Wakefield looked at Elizabeth. "We know you were only trying to help Jessica," he said. "But cutting class, no matter what the reason, isn't something that can be treated lightly."

"You're going to have to worry a little less about Jessica and a little more about yourself from now on," Mrs. Wakefield said quietly.

"Believe me," Elizabeth said sincerely, "I've learned my lesson."

"And remember, you won't always be there to take care of Jessica," Mr. Wakefield reminded her. "Jessica has to learn to be responsible for herself."

"I can't believe it," Elizabeth said. "I never felt so good after getting a talking-to before." She smiled in spite of everything. "I wish I had told you about it much sooner."

Mr. Wakefield leaned back in his chair. "I don't think it would be fair to ground you, but I think you should tell Mr. Clark that you missed the class, too. He can decide what type of punishment you'll have to face. Does that sound fair?"

Elizabeth nodded in agreement.

A few hours later, when Jessica heard Elizabeth was going to turn herself in, she couldn't believe it. "Are you crazy?" she screamed. "After everything we've been through, you want to get yourself into even more trouble." Jessica shook her head. "Why don't you tell Mom and Dad that Mr. Clark didn't give you any punishment. You won't get caught."

Elizabeth would have none of it. "I will never let you talk me into doing anything ever again. I've learned my lesson."

First thing Monday morning, Elizabeth marched into Mr. Clark's office and told him everything she had told her parents. Mr. Clark was shocked.

"I'm surprised at you, Elizabeth," he said. "I can understand your motive, but cutting class is a serious offense. You leave me no choice but to give you the same punishment I gave Jessica and Lila."

Oh, no, Elizabeth groaned to herself. It was going to be a long week.

"I heard you have to stay after school all this week," Amy Sutton said to Elizabeth at lunchtime.

Elizabeth nodded. She was sitting at the table with Amy and Sarah Thomas. They were supposed to be discussing the class project they were working on together. But so far they seemed to be talking about everything else but that.

"You mean you went and squealed on yourself?" Sarah said.

"Well, I wouldn't put it that way," Elizabeth said. Even though no one could believe what she had done, she didn't feel that she had made a mistake. "It was bothering me all week. I think I actually worried myself into feeling sick at one point."

Sarah laughed sarcastically. "I know what you mean," she said. "That's the way I feel every weekend."

Elizabeth shot a look at Amy. She was sorry she had even mentioned the word *weekend*. Ever since she and Amy had teamed up with Sarah in history class, Sarah had made it perfectly clear that weekends weren't her favorite part of the week. In fact it sounded to Elizabeth as though she hated them.

"Anyway," Amy said, trying to fill the awkward

silence, "Brooke told me that Jessica and Lila were bragging to everybody about not squealing on you."

"What?" Elizabeth exclaimed. She couldn't believe those two could possibly try to take credit for that. *The only reason they didn't tell was so Jessica could play in the game!* she thought to herself. "Where did you hear that?"

"When I was standing in the lunch line before," Amy said. "Jessica was right behind me telling Ellen how awful the punishment was and how she did everything she could not to spill the beans about you."

"I heard it from Caroline Pearce," Sarah said. "She was going around telling everyone how loyal and honorable Jessica and Lila were for not telling."

Elizabeth stood up. "I've got to go to my locker," she said. "I'll see you in class."

As Elizabeth stormed through the halls looking for Jessica, she passed Lila and Ellen at the water fountain.

"I wouldn't have done the whole punishment myself," Elizabeth overheard Ellen Riteman say to Lila. "Cleaning blackboards is gross."

"We didn't think it was right to squeal on Elizabeth," Lila said airily. "I don't think I could live with myself if I thought I was a rat!"

Elizabeth stormed away and finally caught up

with Jessica after gym class. "Don't go anywhere," she said to Jessica as they were getting dressed after class. "I need to talk to you."

"I know what it's about," Jessica said with a smile. She picked up the MVP trophy that Ms. Langberg had presented to Elizabeth after class. This time it had Elizabeth's name engraved on the front. "You want to give this to me when no one is around," she whispered.

"I want to give you something all right," Elizabeth said. "But I'm not sure you're going to like it as much as that trophy."

When the twins were finally alone, Jessica picked up the plaque and looked at her reflection in the shiny gold nameplate on the front. "So, Mr. Clark gave you the same punishment I had, huh?" Jessica said sadly. "Too bad. If you had listened to me, you wouldn't be washing blackboards all week."

Elizabeth nodded. "I guess being the loyal sister that you are, you were just looking out for me, huh?"

Jessica smiled.

"So," Elizabeth went on, "since you're so loyal to me, this is how this week's punishment is going to work . . ."

"Oh, I'm sorry, Lizzie," Jessica interrupted. "I just remembered. I've really got to hurry. Lila and Janet are—"

"Oh, no, you don't," Elizabeth said in her older-sister tone. "You're going to stay right here and listen to what I have planned for you."

Jessica stood still. She knew when her sister meant business.

"Now," Elizabeth began sweetly. "Remember how we changed clothes after school last week so you could go to practice and I could clean the blackboards?"

Jessica nodded.

"Well, I'll meet you in the bathroom at three o'clock sharp. I'm sure it will only take a few minutes to change clothes. And don't worry. Washing the blackboards isn't really that difficult—just tiring." She reached over and took the trophy away from Jessica. "I'll make sure this gets put in the right place," she added.

"You mean you're going to take that away from me?" Jessica said.

Elizabeth looked at her name engraved on the front of the award. She pretended to think about it for a second. "Don't worry," she finally said. "I'll put this in your room. I can't deprive you of the trophy, too. Besides, even though it will be in your room, it will always have my name right on the front of it."

Jessica nodded ruefully.

"That's a pretty fair exchange," Elizabeth said. "Don't you think, Jess?"

* * *

Elizabeth walked into Mr. Nydick's history class a few minutes later.

"Where have you been?" Amy whispered. "You're lucky. Mr. Nydick hasn't taken attendance yet."

"I had to talk to Jessica," Elizabeth said. She smiled at Sarah. "Did you come up with any brilliant ideas for the project yet?"

Both girls shook their heads.

"Well, we've got a few more days to think about it," Elizabeth said. "I'm sure we'll come up with something."

"And if we come up with an idea soon, maybe we can work on it this weekend," Amy said.

Elizabeth, remembering how Sarah felt about weekends, glanced over at her. She didn't look very happy.

"Sarah, are you all right?" Elizabeth asked.

"No!" Sarah cried, almost angrily. It looked to Elizabeth as though she might burst into tears. "Just leave me alone, OK?"

Elizabeth was shocked at Sarah's sudden outburst. She couldn't understand how anyone could possibly hate weekends. As Sarah ran from the room, Elizabeth vowed to find out what had upset her so much.

*What's the matter with Sarah Thomas? Find out in Sweet Valley Twins #21, **LEFT BEHIND**.*

THE CLASS TRIP

SWEET VALLEY TWINS SUPER EDITION #1

Join Jessica and Elizabeth in the very first SWEET VALLEY TWINS Super Edition—it's longer, can be read out of sequence, and is full of page-turning excitement!

The day of the big sixth-grade class trip to the Enchanted Forest is finally here! But Jessica and Elizabeth have a fight and spend the beginning of the trip arguing. When Elizabeth decides to make up, Jessica has disappeared. In a frantic search for her sister, Elizabeth finds herself in a series of dangerous and exciting Alice In Wonderland-type of adventures.

☐ 15588-1 $2.95/$3.50 in Canada

Buy them at your local bookstore or use this page to order.

IT ALL STARTED WITH

THE

SWEET VALLEY TWINS

For two years teenagers across the U.S. have been reading about Jessica and Elizabeth Wakefield and their High School friends in SWEET VALLEY HIGH books. Now in books created especially for you, author Francine Pascal introduces you to Jessica and Elizabeth when they were 12, facing the same problems with their folks and friends that you do.